When I Was Little

by Toyomi Igus

illustrated by
Higgins Bond

Printed in the U.S.A. First Edition 10 9 8 7 6 5 4 3
Library of Congress Catalog Number 92-72006
ISBN: 0-940975-32-7 (hardcover) 0-940975-33-5 (paper)

Orange, New Jersey
1992

It was nice where Grandpa Will lived.
It was so quiet, the air smelled so fresh,
and the grass was so green.
Not like where Noel lived in the big city.

Grandpa Will had a house in the country.
And going fishing every summer
—just him and Grandpa—
was Noel's most favorite thing to do.

As they walked toward the river's edge, Grandpa Will looked around, let out a sigh, and said, "Things sure have changed around here."

Noel looked around too, but things sure looked the same to him. Nothing seemed any different from last summer.

"What do you mean, Grandpa?"

"Well, when I was little," Grandpa Will explained, "there were no houses along the river. And there were no fancy docks or condos like those over there.

"Fact is, there was no such thing as a condo. When I was little, there was just this old pier, the river, and plenty of fish."

Noel walked to the end of the dock and tried to imagine
what his grandpa was saying.

Hmmm. The river with just trees. . .and bushes. . .
and no houses. How did the river banks look back then?

"Were there dinosaurs around here when you were little?"
he asked.

Grandpa Will laughed. "No, son, there were no dinosaurs.
The dinosaurs were long gone. But things were different back then.

"Why, when I was little, there was a big old tree over there–you see? Well, that old tree had long, thick branches that hung out over the water. My grandpa used to tie a rope onto one of those branches and we kids would use it for a swing. We used to swing out over the water and jump off—

SPLASH!—right into the river."

"Oooh, that sounds like fun, Grandpa."
Noel wished that the tree was still there so he could try it.
Of course, he'd have to learn how to swim first.

"Yeah, it was a lot of fun," Grandpa said,
"especially on a hot day like today."

Grandpa Will started to fix a hook to the end of Noel's fishing line.

"Did you go swimming every day when you were little, Grandpa?"

"Sure did, son. How else could we keep cool in the summer? See, when I was little, we didn't have air conditioning or even refrigerators."

No refrigerators? Noel found this hard to believe.

"How did you keep ice cream frozen or the milk and soda cold?"

"Well, when I was little, Mama used to send us kids
down to the store with a quarter to buy a big block of ice.
The ice man would put it in our wagon and we'd drag it home.
Mama would put the ice in the ice box to keep our food cold.
But the best part was sucking on the little chips of ice
that Mama would let us keep."

"Boy, Grandpa, that sounds like fun, too."

Noel tried to imagine going to the store to buy ice.
There was a lot of traffic where he lived, so his mother wouldn't
let him go to the store to buy anything!
Not 'til he was bigger anyway.

"Sounds like fun, huh? Well, maybe so, but it was still
another chore to us. Boy, it seemed like
we had a million chores to do when I was little—
hauling ice, tending the garden, washing clothes. . ."

"Oh, I know what you did, Grandpa.
I've seen it on TV. You had to wash your clothes
in the river, right? Like the pioneers."

"Kind of like that," Grandpa Will smiled.
"'Cept we had to help Mama scrub the clothes on
a washboard in a big tub. Mama would rub the clothes
up and down, up and down, 'til they were clean.
Then we'd hang them out on the line to dry in the sun."

As his grandpa talked, Noel tried to figure out how
people washed their clothes by hand on a board. He and
his mother always did their laundry at the corner laundromat.
All they had to do was put their clothes in a washing machine
and the machine did all the work.

"Grandpa, what else was different when you were little?" asked Noel.

Grandpa Will pulled a worm out of his can and started to bait Noel's fishing line. Noel watched him carefully. One day he was going to learn to do that.

"Well," Grandpa said. "When I was little, do you know that we didn't even have a telephone?"

"What!?"

Noel couldn't imagine that. Without a phone,
how could he call his mom from Grandpa's house?
Or talk to Grandpa Will when he went home?
How could he talk to his best friend, Jojo,
who lived four whole blocks away?

Grandpa Will saw the confused look on Noel's face
and laughed again.

"No, what I mean, son, is that telephones were invented,
but only rich people could afford to buy them. My family
didn't have one.

"I remember Miz Johnson down the street had a phone,
and she'd let us use it in an emergency. Telephones
looked a lot different back then too. When I was little,
we didn't have all these fancy colors and push buttons.
Most of the phones were black and they had what you call
rotary dials—or no dials at all."

"Then how did you talk to people, Grandpa?"

"Why we'd write letters or send telegrams to people
who were far away. And if our friends weren't far way,
well, then we'd just go and visit them.

"People did a lot more of that in those days—
visitin' folks, I mean. In the evening after work
and school, there wasn't much else to do.
We didn't have television, so it seemed like
we had a lot more time on our hands."

"You didn't have TV either, Grandpa? No cartoons?
Boy, that must have been awful."

"No, Noel, it wasn't awful. You can't miss what you never had. The grown-ups would sit on the porch after dinner and talk, while we kids would run around trying to catch lightin' bugs.

"Sometimes we'd all gather in the living room and listen to the radio. Radio was our TV when I was little. We'd listen to the comedy shows and just laugh and have a good time.

"Or sometimes Uncle Hoot would pull out his Fats Waller records and play music on the phonograph.
A phonograph is a record player—like a CD player—
but when I was little, you had to wind it up to make it go."

Noel loved to dance, so he thought life might not be so bad without a TV, as long as he had his music. He could almost see it—grandpa dancing and Uncle Hoot being the deejay.

Hmmm. Fats Waller. Noel wondered if he was a rapper. He asked his grandpa.

Grandpa Will let out a big belly laugh and hugged Noel. "Was Fats Waller a rapper? Well, in a way, I guess he was."

The two fishermen lowered their lines into the calm, clear water. They breathed in the fresh green smell of the river, and they waited for the fish to bite.

Suddenly the stillness was broken by the sound of a jet plane flying overhead.

Noel looked up. He had flown on a plane just like that to come and visit his grandpa.

"I bet you didn't have airplanes either when you were little, right, Grandpa?"

Grandpa Will looked up too.
"Well, we did but . . .

Noel interrupted. "When *you* were little . . ."

Grandpa smiled.

"Yep. When I was little the planes were smaller and had propellers in the front to help them go. And they made a lot of noise! But you're right, son. There were no jet planes, and no rockets or space shuttles either.

"When people went somewhere they mostly traveled on trains. Here in the country, though, we rode on wagons pulled by our horses."

"What about cars? Didn't you have cars when you were little?" Noel asked.

"Oh, some folks had cars, but most of us couldn't afford them back then.

"I remember the first time I rode in an automobile. It was a Model A and the car belonged to Reverend Gibbs.

"Once when I stayed late after Sunday school the Reverend took me home in his brand-new automobile. Boy, was I excited!

"The automobile was all new and shiny and smelled like leather. I got in and he started up the car.

"Let me tell you, I was never so scared in all my life! We were going so *fast!* And the car was so *noisy!*"

"Yessir, you have a lot of things now that we didn't have
when I was little. No jets, no cars. No washing machines
or driers. No televisions, or VCRs, or video games. No cassette tapes,
CDs, or stereos.

"Why, when I was little, we didn't even have indoor toilets.
We had to go outside to the outhouse to go to the bathroom.
Boy, did I hate going to the bathroom in the middle of the night—
in the dark and the cold, through snow or rain. That old outhouse
was the scariest place at night!"

Grandpa Will laughed at the memory. Life really was different when he was little.

Noel watched the river current pull and tug on his fishing line and thought about everything his grandfather told him.

He thought about how much fun it would have been to go swinging into the river.

He wondered if the ice they put into grandpa's ice box tasted any different from the ice cubes he got from the freezer.

And he thought it would really be neat to travel around in horse-drawn wagons.

But what would life *really* be like without refrigerators and televisions? Without spaceships and rockets, VCRs and video games? Without indoor toilets? Noel couldn't imagine having to go the bathroom alone in the cold and the dark.

Finally he said, "Grandpa, it sounds like you had a lot of fun, but I think I'm glad *I* wasn't little when *you* were little."

Suddenly Noel's fishing line pulled tight.
Grandpa Will helped Noel quickly reel in his line.
A big old crappie was dangling off the other end of it.

"Look, Grandpa!" Noel said excitedly.
"Look! I caught one! I caught one!"

Noel struggled to hold onto the wiggling fish that looked almost as big as he was.

Grandpa Will smiled, remembering his own first catch.

"Things sure are different now," he said, hugging his grandson,
"but it's good to see that the important things are still the same."